ND YOU
Y MERCER MAYER

*To Caleb and
Justine McNair
with love*

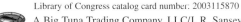

HarperFestival
A Division of HarperCollins Publishers

Today in school we learned about what foods are good for us.

I asked why carrots are better for me than cookies.

"Because carrots have vitamins to help you grow," Miss Kitty told me. "Cookies just taste good."

In gym, we did lots of exercises. First, we jumped rope. I jumped the fastest, but the rope was a little too long.

We had a contest to see who could do the most sit-ups and push-ups. I won—almost.

The next day, I made lunch for Mom, Dad, and Little Sister.

"Surprise!" I said. "Eat every bite, because all of this food is good for you."

After lunch, I told my family I had another surprise. I took them all on a bike ride.
"Come on, Dad!" I said. "You can do it!"

The next day when Tiger came over to play
video games, I had a great idea.

The next morning, I walked to school instead of taking the bus. I had to hurry because walking sure takes longer.

I called all of our friends
to tell them.

At lunch, I almost had a brownie for dessert,
but I decided to have an apple instead.

On the way home, we saw a big sign.

"Look," said Gabby. "There's going to be a race in Critterville."

"Let's run in the race!" I said.

Everybody cheered.

Gabby said we should do
exercises to get ready for the race.
But then I got hungry, so I
stopped to have a snack.

Tiger and Malcolm were hungry, too, so I gave each
of them a snack. Exercise sure gives you a big appetite.

The next day, we went swimming. I wore my snorkel and my flippers because they make me go faster.

After that, we practiced running as fast as we could.
I beat Tiger . . .

. . . but Gator beat me.

Malcolm beat all three of us . . .

. . . but Gabby beat Malcolm. Gabby's really fast.

The day of the race, we all took our places at the starting line.

"On your marks, get set, go!" called the announcer.
Then he blew a whistle.

I got off to a fast start.

I didn't win, but I ran the whole way without stopping. Doing stuff that's good for you isn't just healthy, it's lots of fun, too.